Minnesota

Wisconsin

Michigan

Vermont

New York

New Hampshire

Massachusetts

Iowa

Illinois

Indiana

Ohio

Pennsylvania

Rhode Island

Connecticut

New Jersey

Delaware

Maryland

Washington, D.C.

West Virginia

Virginia

Missouri

Kentucky

North Carolina

klahoma

Arkansas

Tennessee

South Carolina

Mississippi

Alabama

Georgia

Louisiana

Florida

N

W

E

S

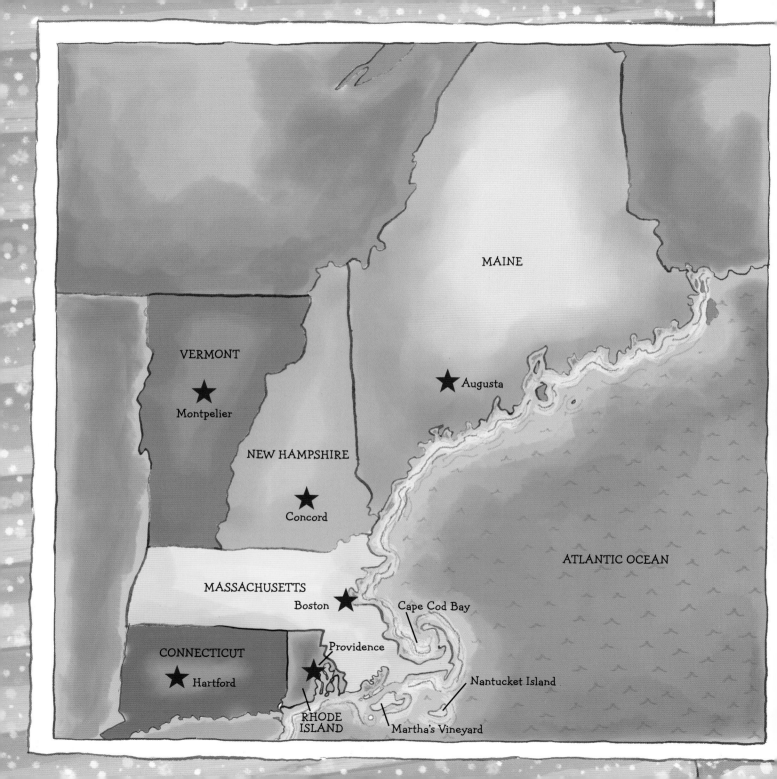

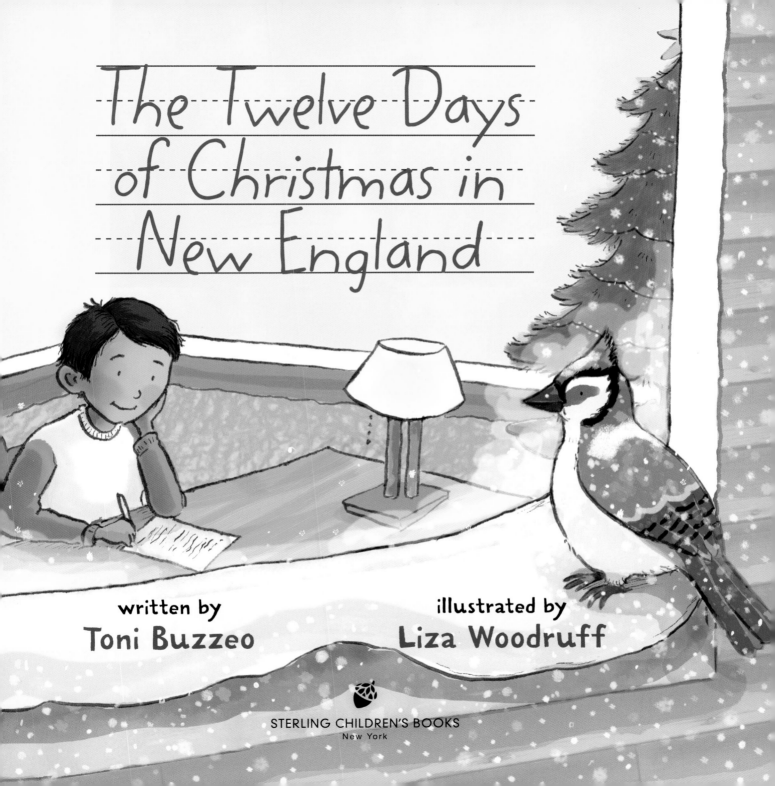

# The Twelve Days of Christmas in New England

written by
## Toni Buzzeo

illustrated by
## Liza Woodruff

STERLING CHILDREN'S BOOKS
New York

Dear Grace,

Pack your bags, Cousin! Mom, Dad, and I are so excited to share **ALL** of New England with you over Christmas vacation. We're going to have six states' worth of fun, spending two days in each state. Can you name them all? Of course **I** can, because I live here. From the shortest name to the longest, they are: Maine, Vermont, Rhode Island, Connecticut, New Hampshire, and Massachusetts.

Wait until you see all the places we have planned to visit, from the biggest city, Boston, to the tiniest coastal and mountain towns. To save time, we'll fly around in Mom's helicopter and rent a car when we need one. From lighthouse hopping to moose spotting, it's going to be a trip you'll never forget!

We're having a "real" New England winter this year, so you'd better pack a parka, snow pants, and boots. Mom says, "Tell Grace that I'm knitting her a matching scarf, hat, and mittens set, and a pile of wool socks!" Now you know what you're getting for Christmas from her. But you'll **NEVER** guess what you're getting from me. Just be prepared for a different surprise each of the twelve days of Christmas.

See you soon!

Your favorite cousin,

Camden

Dear Mom and Dad,

Squawk! I wish you didn't have to wait eleven days to meet Squawky, the blue jay Camden gave me today along with my very own black spruce tree. Did you know that black spruce trees and blue jays live in every New England state? Squawky will feel right at home as we travel!

Aunt Caitlin, Uncle Christopher, and Camden met me at Logan Airport. Then we hopped on the "T" (that's Boston's mass transit system) to Boston Common, the oldest public park in the United States. There, a 50-foot-tall black spruce tree, a gift from Nova Scotia, waited right next to MY tree from Camden. Mine is only a baby now, but just wait.

Wow! Boston is packed with history. Have you heard of the Freedom Trail and the Black Heritage Trail? We walked on parts of both today. I was actually INSIDE Paul Revere's house! It's the oldest building in downtown Boston (nearly 340 years old). I got shivers thinking of Paul taking his midnight ride to warn the patriots that the British soldiers were coming. Long ago, abolitionist Frederick Douglass gave an anti-slavery speech in the African Meeting House we visited today. Isn't that amazing? Suddenly, history is alive.

By the time we gobbled up all that history, it was dark (and cold). But that didn't stop Aunt Caitlin from flying us out to Cape Cod in her helicopter so we could collect shells on the beach by moonlight. So far, Massachusetts is magical!

Your New England shell-seeker,

Grace

Dear Mom and Dad,

Did you notice the butterfly stickers all over my envelope? Now imagine REAL butterflies of every pattern and color at the Magic Wings Butterfly Conservatory in South Deerfield, Massachusetts. We arrived all bundled up in our parkas but walked right into tropical summer in the conservatory. Thousands of butterflies fluttered around us as we strolled through an enchanted world of tropical plants, reptiles, and birds. (Squawky was really mad that we'd left him behind.) My favorite part was the feeling of butterflies landing with a soft tickle to hitchhike a ride on my hands. And I love the pair of wings Camden found for me in the gift shop!

After a short helicopter hop, we landed in Springfield, where we waved a quick hello to the gigantic Horton, Lorax, and Cat in the Hat in the Dr. Seuss National Memorial Sculpture Garden. Then we headed off to the Basketball Hall of Fame. Who knew that basketball was born in Springfield? Camden and I had so much fun at the rebound drill. So, we staged a hoops competition on the full-size court. Too bad he didn't know about the hoop on our garage. Guess who won?

A visit to Plimoth Plantation (remember the Pilgrims?) was the perfect end to our day. As we walked through the door of the old Grist Mill, holly and ivy, ringing sleigh bells, roasted chestnuts, hot cider, and gingerbread waited for us.

Your New England sugarplum,
Grace

On the second day of Christmas,
my cousin gave to me . . .

2 gauzy wings

and a blue jay in a spruce tree.

Dear Mom and Dad,

A new day, a new state! New Hampshire is right next door to Massachusetts (and to Maine and Vermont too), so we flew up to Concord right after breakfast.

Do you think of rockets and space when you think of New England? I sure didn't, but the McAuliffe-Shepard Discovery Center, named after two New Hampshirites, Christa McAuliffe, the first teacher in space, and Alan Shepard, the first American in space, changed my mind! I might even want to be an astronaut one day. Do you think you could land a space shuttle or a lunar lander? Thanks to a really cool flight simulator, I got to do both! Between the planetarium show and viewing blazing sunspots through a giant telescope, Camden and I are brand-new space buffs.

"Dashing through the snow, in a one-horse open sleigh." The song sure came to life during our afternoon adventure! Imagine an enormous chestnut-colored draft horse pulling an old-fashioned black sleigh on shining runners. I felt like I'd stepped into a movie scene. A light dusting of snow landed on us as we raced across acres of glistening white.

Our sleigh ride put us in the perfect mood for our evening candlelight stroll at Strawbery Banke in Portsmouth. Music swirled around us as we walked through lantern-lit lanes and into historic houses filled with handmade decorations. More New England magic!

Your astronaut-in-training,
Grace

On the third day of Christmas, my cousin gave to me . . .

3 swift sleighs

2 gauzy wings, and a blue jay in a spruce tree.

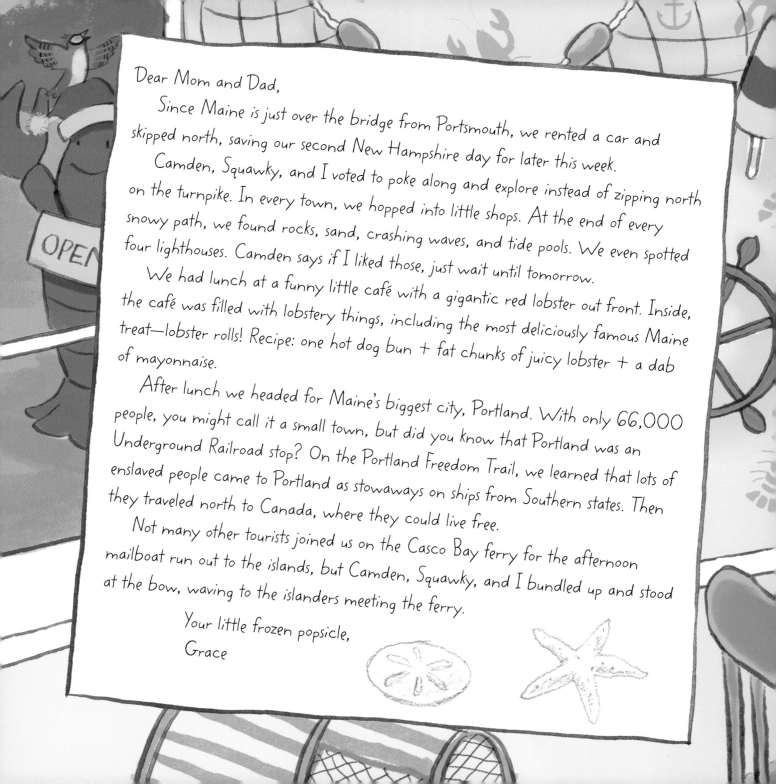

Dear Mom and Dad,

Since Maine is just over the bridge from Portsmouth, we rented a car and skipped north, saving our second New Hampshire day for later this week.

Camden, Squawky, and I voted to poke along and explore instead of zipping north on the turnpike. In every town, we hopped into little shops. At the end of every snowy path, we found rocks, sand, crashing waves, and tide pools. We even spotted four lighthouses. Camden says if I liked those, just wait until tomorrow.

We had lunch at a funny little café with a gigantic red lobster out front. Inside, the café was filled with lobstery things, including the most deliciously famous Maine treat—lobster rolls! Recipe: one hot dog bun + fat chunks of juicy lobster + a dab of mayonnaise.

After lunch we headed for Maine's biggest city, Portland. With only 66,000 people, you might call it a small town, but did you know that Portland was an Underground Railroad stop? On the Portland Freedom Trail, we learned that lots of enslaved people came to Portland as stowaways on ships from Southern states. Then they traveled north to Canada, where they could live free.

Not many other tourists joined us on the Casco Bay ferry for the afternoon mailboat run out to the islands, but Camden, Squawky, and I bundled up and stood at the bow, waving to the islanders meeting the ferry.

Your little frozen popsicle,
Grace

On the fourth day of Christmas,
my cousin gave to me . . .

4 lobster rolls

3 swift sleighs, 2 gauzy wings,
and a blue jay in a spruce tree.

Dear Mom and Dad,

Camden promised a "lighthouse day," and he sure came through! Five golden beams were today's gifts, so start counting. At daybreak, we arrived in Cape Elizabeth at the oldest lighthouse in Maine. George Washington had Portland Head Light built, and poet Henry Wadsworth Longfellow took lots of long walks from Portland to visit it.

In Boothbay, we spotted Burnt Island Lighthouse, a living history museum just offshore. If only it weren't winter, we could have ferried to the island to learn about early life there. The tour guides dress up just like a real lighthouse family!

I'm sending you a Maine quarter so you can see Pemaquid Point Lighthouse, too. The white tower, shining in the sunlight above cascading rocks, dazzled me. Luckily, I packed my sunglasses.

I could practically hear "Spot" barking at Owls Head Light. People say that the keeper's dog pulled the fog bell rope with his teeth whenever a ship entered Rockland Harbor.

Our last lighthouse was Rockland Breakwater Light. Its red brick tower sits at the end of a man-made wall protecting the harbor. The breakwater was built with <u>700,000</u> tons of granite and stretches almost a mile. Luckily, we packed our walking shoes!

After all that sightseeing, Camden and I were ready for some action on Mount Desert Island. We wrapped our scarves over our noses and mouths, strapped on helmets, and climbed on borrowed snowmobiles—Uncle Christopher and Aunt Caitlin drove. We bounced along the 27-mile Acadia National Park Loop Road until sunset.

Your lighthouse-loving daughter,
Grace

# On the fifth day of Christmas, my cousin gave to me . . .

ROCKLAND BREAKWATER

OWLS HEAD

PEMAQUID POINT

BURNT ISLAND

5 golden beams

**4** lobster rolls, **3** swift sleighs, **2** gauzy wings, and a blue jay in a spruce tree.

Dear Mom and Dad,

I'm naming today—our second day in snowy New Hampshire—triple-vehicle-transport day. We started in the helicopter, flying to a dogsled touring kennel in White Mountain National Forest where we were introduced to our second vehicles—dogsleds! Imagine a chorus of 100 barking, whining, howling huskies and malamutes all welcoming us and begging, WOOF! WOOF-WOOF! ("Hello! Pick me!")

With six dogs harnessed and hitched, Camden and I boarded our sled. We were all bundled up, but despite three pairs of wool socks, my toes nearly froze. It's COLD out on the trail—so cold the packed snow squeaked under the flying sled as we spotted Mount Washington, New England's highest mountain!

Camden and I each took a turn driving our sled with Jane, our musher (that's what they call sled drivers). It was a lot harder than it looks, at least for me. Camden was a natural, knowing just when to brake to slow the sled and just how to lean into a turn. We both loved the commands: "Gee!" (turn right), "Haw!" (turn left), and "Whoa!" (stop).

After all of that fresh air, we were definitely ready for our third vehicle of the day—a rented Jeep for our tour of Moose Alley! They say there are about 10,000 moose living here. I wasn't feeling greedy, though. One would do. And Squawky and I were the first to spot one—a big bull moose. I bet you didn't know that moose don't have antlers in winter!

     Your moose-spotting musher,
     Grace

On the sixth day of Christmas,
my cousin gave to me . . .

6 dogs a-mushing

5 golden beams, 4 lobster rolls,
3 swift sleighs, 2 gauzy wings,
and a blue jay in a spruce tree.

Dear Mom and Dad,

Northeast Kingdom, Vermont—isn't that the coolest name? I've always wanted to visit a kingdom! Of course, there's no king or queen, just rolling snow-covered hills and millions of trees. We visited an amazing place there—the Bread and Puppet Museum, which is usually closed in winter, but Uncle Christopher made a special appointment so we could take a private tour.

Way back in 1963, Peter Schumann started the Bread and Puppet Theater in New York City. Now, there are summer performances, with Peter's fresh-baked rye bread, at his home in Glover, Vermont. The museum, a 150-year-old barn, is full to the rafters—two stories high—of ENORMOUS puppets and masks from over 50 years of shows. Camden loved the masks—so huge and strong but gentle at the same time. My favorite was a puppet that looked just like Nonna, sitting at her machine, happily sewing. I HAVE to take you there someday—you'd love it.

Aunt Caitlin says you can't visit Vermont without a tour of the Ben & Jerry's ice cream factory in Waterbury and a creamy, chunky, triple-scoop cone. One good thing about winter—no dripping cones when wandering through the outdoor Flavor Graveyard, a funny cemetery with tombstones for "retired" ice cream flavors.

Camden and I ended our day on a hill with a long, slick slope, racing each other on super speedy sleds under the lights. Score: 4-4.

Your peanut-butter-chocolate-chip-coconut-cashew fan,
Grace

Dear Mom and Dad,

Christmas trees! You know how we just pick out the best tree in that crowded lot in town? Wait until you hear what we've been missing. Vermont is famous for its nearly one thousand dairy farms, but my new favorite kind of Vermont farm is a <u>Christmas tree</u> farm!

Imagine a light snow falling on gently rolling hills. Straight rows of dark green balsam and Fraser fir trees stand like tin soldiers as far as you can see. Squawky immediately chose his favorite and perched on top. The delicious spicy smell of evergreens filled the air as families cut their own trees. I wonder if OUR Christmas tree ever came from Vermont?

Of course, you can't visit Vermont without skiing. Vermont has the longest ski trails in New England. ("Vertical drop" is how you measure the length of ski slopes from top to base.) I took a lesson for beginners and caught on right away. It must be in my genes! Then Camden and I rode the ski lift and watched the skiers below carving and schussing. Pretty soon, I got to join them.

Uncle Christopher says one of the best parts of a day on the slopes is hot chocolate by the fire in the lodge when you're bone-tired and happy, like I am now.

Your sleepy ski bunny,
Grace

On the eighth day of Christmas,
my cousin gave to me . . .

8 skiers carving

7 puppets smiling, 6 dogs a-mushing, 5 golden beams,
4 lobster rolls, 3 swift sleighs, 2 gauzy wings,
and a blue jay in a spruce tree.

Dear Mom and Dad,

The ninth day of Christmas was ANIMAL DAY. First stop, the Beardsley Zoo in Bridgeport, Connecticut (my fifth New England state). The zoo was started in the same park where the famous circus master, P. T. Barnum, used to exercise his circus animals. Aside from the carousel, my favorite exhibits were the South American rainforest, with boa constrictors, black howler monkeys, and vampire bats, and the prairie dog habitat. Camden, Squawky, and I crawled through the underground tunnels and popped up in plexiglass tubes right next to the prairie dogs. Best zoo fun ever!

Our next stop was the Yale Peabody Museum of Natural History in New Haven. Camden and I decided to visit the Discovery Room. Know why? Because its most important rule is PLEASE TOUCH! I got to touch a one-hundred-million-year-old fossil. Meanwhile, Camden spotted all sixteen live poison dart frogs, being such an expert after checking out the rainforest exhibit at the zoo.

Last but so very NOT least, we flew to the Mystic Aquarium. I officially fell in love with penguins at a Penguin Encounter! Picture this: Camden and I sat with others in a circle while a friendly little African penguin walked around greeting us. We touched her soft feathers, talked to her, and asked her trainer all kinds of questions. Best of all, she held still while I listened to her heartbeat with a stethoscope! Just as we were saying goodbye, Camden surprised me with nine African penguins of my own. You'd better stock up on fish!

Your penguin-petting daughter,
Grace

Dear Mom and Dad,

I was prepared for New England to be ENORMOUSLY fun. But I didn't know it was also the home of ENORMOUS prehistoric animals until we flew to Rocky Hill, Connecticut, to visit Dinosaur State Park. As we followed 500 fossilized tracks under a geodesic dome built to protect them, Camden, Squawky, and I went wild imagining what the dinosaurs would have looked like. But most scientists agree that all the tracks were made by 20-foot-long carnivores weighing 1,000 pounds each.

I bet you didn't know that fossil tracks are named separately from the animals that created them. So all of these tracks are named Eubrontes—the official Connecticut State Fossil!

After a morning of science, we flew off to the Mark Twain House & Museum in Hartford. Mark Twain (otherwise known as Samuel Clemens) wasn't just a great author of books like The Adventures of Huckleberry Finn and The Adventures of Tom Sawyer, he was also a big fan of billiards (we call it "pool" nowadays). The Billiard Room, where Twain wrote his books AND played pool, was my favorite. If only I could have challenged Camden to a game of billiards, I know I would have won!

Our day ended at Goodwin Park with the Holiday Light Fantasia. The Fantasia is a two-mile drive through a wonderland of over one million Christmas lights. And you thought OUR Christmas lights were great, Dad!

Your pool shark,
Grace

On the eighth day of Christmas,
my cousin gave to me . . .

8 skiers carving

**7** puppets smiling, **6** dogs a-mushing, **5** golden beams,
**4** lobster rolls, **3** swift sleighs, **2** gauzy wings,
and a blue jay in a spruce tree.

Dear Mom and Dad,

The ninth day of Christmas was ANIMAL DAY. First stop, the Beardsley Zoo in Bridgeport, Connecticut (my fifth New England state). The zoo was started in the same park where the famous circus master, P. T. Barnum, used to exercise his circus animals. Aside from the carousel, my favorite exhibits were the South American rainforest, with boa constrictors, black howler monkeys, and vampire bats, and the prairie dog habitat. Camden, Squawky, and I crawled through the underground tunnels and popped up in plexiglass tubes right next to the prairie dogs. Best zoo fun ever!

Our next stop was the Yale Peabody Museum of Natural History in New Haven. Camden and I decided to visit the Discovery Room. Know why? Because its most important rule is PLEASE TOUCH! I got to touch a one-hundred-million-year-old fossil. Meanwhile, Camden spotted all sixteen live poison dart frogs, being such an expert after checking out the rainforest exhibit at the zoo.

Last but so very NOT least, we flew to the Mystic Aquarium. I officially fell in love with penguins at a Penguin Encounter! Picture this: Camden and I sat with others in a circle while a friendly little African penguin walked around greeting us. We touched her soft feathers, talked to her, and asked her trainer all kinds of questions. Best of all, she held still while I listened to her heartbeat with a stethoscope! Just as we were saying goodbye, Camden surprised me with nine African penguins of my own. You'd better stock up on fish!

Your penguin-petting daughter,
Grace

On the tenth day of Christmas,
my cousin gave to me . . .

10 dinos roaming

9 penguins playing, 8 skiers carving,
7 puppets smiling, 6 dogs a-mushing, 5 golden beams,
4 lobster rolls, 3 swift sleighs, 2 gauzy wings,
and a blue jay in a spruce tree.

Dear Mom and Dad,

We arrived in the last state on our New England tour today. Rhode Island may be the smallest state, but it's got a very big art museum! Imagine more than 84,000 objects in five buildings—that's the RISD (Rhode Island School of Design) Museum of Art. We tried to see every single thing. I would never be able to tell you about them all, but my favorites were the ancient Greek artifacts, especially the beautiful bronze helmet from around 500 CE. Camden wanted to try it on, but I talked him out of it. All of the art created by RISD students might have changed my mind about my future career again!

We could have spent the whole day wandering through the five buildings, but you know I get restless if I'm inside for too long. Aunt Caitlin probably knows that too, because she suggested skating—and I don't mean roller-skating either! Everyone else had their own ice skates packed—even Squawky—but my rented pair fit perfectly. They may have had a little magic in them too because I only fell twice before I got the hang of gliding across the HUGE Providence Rink. (It's twice the size of the rink at Rockefeller Center in New York City!) By the end of the afternoon, I was even able to do some wobbly spins. Maybe I have a future in Olympic figure skating!

Your ice dancer,
Grace

On the eleventh day of Christmas,
my cousin gave to me . . .

11 skaters gliding

10 dinos roaming, 9 penguins playing, 8 skiers carving,
7 puppets smiling, 6 dogs a-mushing, 5 golden beams,
4 lobster rolls, 3 swift sleighs, 2 gauzy wings,
and a blue jay in a spruce tree.

Dear Mom and Dad,

My last day! Aunt Caitlin made a special appointment with the museum director at the Tomaquag Indian Memorial Museum in Exeter. This is the only museum in Rhode Island operated by Native people. You may not know much about the Narragansett Indian Tribe yet, but wait until I get home—I'll tell you all about them. They are descended from the aboriginal people who lived here thousands of years ago. The Eastern Woodland Basket Exhibit was my favorite, of course, because of my basketmaking class last summer. What beautiful baskets and birchbark containers. I especially liked a little woven ash basket with curly splints in a strawberry shape. Awesome!

Lastly, in Newport we toured the Newport Mansions. Wow! The ten historic house museums were "summer cottages" of the richest people in America, built by famous architects in the 1800s and 1900s. Each one has its own style, and at Christmastime, The Breakers, The Elms, and Marble House are decorated and open to visitors like us. Squawky looked great perched on the red and white poinsettias on every staircase. And Dad, we may have too many Christmas decorations, but we'd never have enough to decorate the 28 trees I counted! Best of all, though, were the GHOSTS we saw! Aunt Caitlin and Uncle Christopher said we were imagining things, but Camden and I are SURE we counted a dozen ghosts as we toured the mansions.

I already miss New England, but can't wait to show you all the gifts Camden gave me. Maybe you could rent a really big truck to pick me up at the airport?

Your ghost hunter,
Grace

On the twelfth day of Christmas,
my cousin gave to me...

12 ghosts a-haunting

11 skaters gliding, 10 dinos roaming, 9 penguins playing,
8 skiers carving, 7 puppets smiling, 6 dogs a-mushing, 5 golden beams,
4 lobster rolls, 3 swift sleighs, 2 gauzy wings,
and a blue jay in a spruce tree.

# Connecticut: The Constitution State

**Capital:** Hartford • **State Bird:** the American robin • **State Flower:** the mountain laurel
**State Tree:** the white oak • **State Motto:** *Qui Transtulit Sustinet* "He Who Transplanted Still Sustains"

# Maine: The Pine Tree State

**Capital:** Augusta • **State Bird:** the chickadee • **State Flower:** the white pine cone
**State Tree:** the white pine • **State Motto:** *Dirigo* "I Lead"

# Massachusetts: The Bay State

**Capital:** Boston • **State Bird:** the black-capped chickadee • **State Flower:** the Mayflower
**State Tree:** the American elm • **State Motto:** *Ense petit placidam sub libertate quietem*
"By the Sword We Seek Peace, but Peace Only Under Liberty"

# New Hampshire: The Granite State

**Capital:** Concord • **State Bird:** the purple finch • **State Flower:** the purple lilac
**State Tree:** the white birch • **State Motto:** "Live Free or Die"

# Rhode Island: The Ocean State

**Capital:** Providence • **State Bird:** the Rhode Island red • **State Flower:** the violet
**State Tree:** the red maple • **State Motto:** "Hope"

# Vermont: The Green Mountain State

**Capital:** Montpelier • **State Bird:** the hermit thrush • **State Flower:** the red clover
**State Tree:** the sugar maple • **State Motto:** "Freedom and Unity"

**Some Famous New Englanders:**

**Ethan Allen** (1738–1789) was a Revolutionary War patriot, hero, and one of the founders of the Green Mountain Boys, Patriot militiamen, as well as the state of Vermont.

**Susan B. Anthony** (1820–1906) was born in Massachusetts and became one of the leading women in the fight for women's right to vote.

**Crispus Attucks** (c.1723–1770), killed in the Boston Massacre, was the first casualty of the American Revolution. He was a Massachusetts seaman of African and Native American descent.

**John Chapman** (c.1774–1845), the first official folk hero of Massachusetts, was known as Johnny Appleseed because he planted apple trees from New England to the Ohio River Valley.

**Joseph Cinqué** (c.1814–c.1879), a West African, was the top defendant in the Connecticut court case United States v. The Amistad. He and 51 others were found to have been victims of the illegal Atlantic slave trade.

**Dorothy Canfield Fisher** (1879–1958) was a Vermont author of children's and adult books who held a doctorate degree and was the first woman to serve on the State Board of Education.

**Robert Frost** (1874–1963), a famous New Hampshire poet who wrote poems that reflected the life and landscape of New England, won four Pulitzer Prizes.

**Sarah Josepha Hale** (1788–1879) was born in New Hampshire and became a famous author and journalist who campaigned for the establishment of Thanksgiving and who wrote "Mary Had a Little Lamb."

**Anne Hutchinson** (1591–1643) was an early advocate for religious freedom and free speech. She was the first woman to participate in the founding of a town in America—Portsmouth, Rhode Island.

**Henry Wadsworth Longfellow** (1807–1882), who was born in Maine, is considered one of America's best-loved poets with works such as "The Song of Hiawatha."

**Metacomet (King Philip)** (c.1638–1676), chief (or sachem) of the Wampanoag Indians in Rhode Island and Massachusetts, led his people in King Philip's War, an uprising against English colonists in New England.

**Margaret Chase Smith** (1897–1995), born in Maine, became the first woman to serve in both houses of Congress and the first woman to run for presidential nomination.

**Andrew Sockalexis** (1892–1919), a runner from Maine, participated in the 1912 Olympics hosted by Sweden and was quoted as saying that he was running not only for the United States but also for his own people, the Penobscot Indians.

**Harriet Beecher Stowe** (1811–1896) was a Connecticut author of more than thirty books, including the best-selling *Uncle Tom's Cabin*, an anti-slavery novel.

**Daisy Turner** (1883–1988) was a Vermont storyteller and poet, one of thirteen children born to former slaves. She is known for her tales about her family's history, which could be traced back three generations to Africa.

**Prince Whipple** (1750–1796), a Revolutionary War veteran who lived in Portsmouth, New Hampshire, was an African-American slave and later freedman. He is pictured as the soldier seated in front of George Washington in the famous painting *Washington Crossing the Delaware*, although he was not present at Trenton during the crossing.

**Eli Whitney** (1765–1825) was a Connecticut inventor who patented the cotton gin, a key invention of the Industrial Revolution.

**Roger Williams** (c.1603–1683) purchased land from the Narragansett Indians and founded the first permanent white settlement in Rhode Island at Providence in 1636.

To the real Caitlin, Christopher, and Camden. I will always choose to spend
my twelve days of Christmas with you!

Thanks to two online professional communities for their suggestions
on the journey: NESCBWI and LM_NET. —T. B.

To Sara. —L. W.

STERLING CHILDREN'S BOOKS
New York

An Imprint of Sterling Publishing
1166 Avenue of the Americas
New York, NY 10036

Text © 2015 by Toni Buzzeo
Illustrations © 2015 by Liza Woodruff
The artwork for this book was created with pen and ink, and digital paint, pencil, and pastel.
Designed by Andrea Miller
Ben & Jerry's® is a registered trademark of Ben & Jerry's Homemade, Inc. All rights reserved.

ISBN 978-1-4549-1492-1

Distributed in Canada by Sterling Publishing
c/o Canadian Manda Group, 664 Annette Street
Toronto, Ontario, Canada M6S 2C8
Distributed in the United Kingdom by GMC Distribution Services
Castle Place, 166 High Street, Lewes, East Sussex, England BN7 1XU
Distributed in Australia by Capricorn Link (Australia) Pty. Ltd.
P.O. Box 704, Windsor, NSW 2756, Australia

For information about custom editions, special sales, and premium and corporate purchases,
please contact Sterling Special Sales at 800-805-5489 or specialsales@sterlingpublishing.com.

Manufactured in China
Lot #:
2 4 6 8 10 9 7 5 3 1
07/15

www.sterlingpublishing.com/kids